This book belongs to

. . . .

Front endpapers by Kieran Rivers aged 7
Back endpapers by Bethany Crosbie aged 11
Thank you to Dunmore Primary School, Abingdon, Oxfordshire
for helping with the endpapers – K.P.
For Helen Mortimer – V.T.
For Molly Dallas – K.P.

OXFORD
UNIVERSITY PRESS

Great Clarendon Street, Oxford OX2 6DP

Oxford University Press is a department of the University of Oxford.
It furthers the University's objective of excellence in research, scholarship,
and education by publishing worldwide in

Oxford New York

Auckland Cape Town Dar es Salaam Hong Kong Karachi
Kuala Lumpur Madrid Melbourne Mexico City Nairobi
New Delhi Shanghai Taipei Toronto

With offices in

Argentina Austria Brazil Chile Czech Republic France Greece
Guatemala Hungary Italy Japan Poland Portugal Singapore
South Korea Switzerland Thailand Turkey Ukraine Vietnam

Oxford is a registered trade mark of Oxford University Press
in the UK and in certain other countries

First published 2010

8 10 9 7

British Library Cataloguing in Publication Data available

ISBN: 978-0-19-273218-7 (hardback)
ISBN: 978-0-19-273219-4 (paperback)
ISBN: 978-0-19-273220-0 (paperback with audio CD)

Printed in China

Paper used in the production of this book is a natural, recyclable product made
from wood grown in sustainable forests. The manufacturing process conforms to the
environmental regulations of the country of origin

www.winnie-the-witch.com

Valerie Thomas and Korky Paul

Winnie in Space

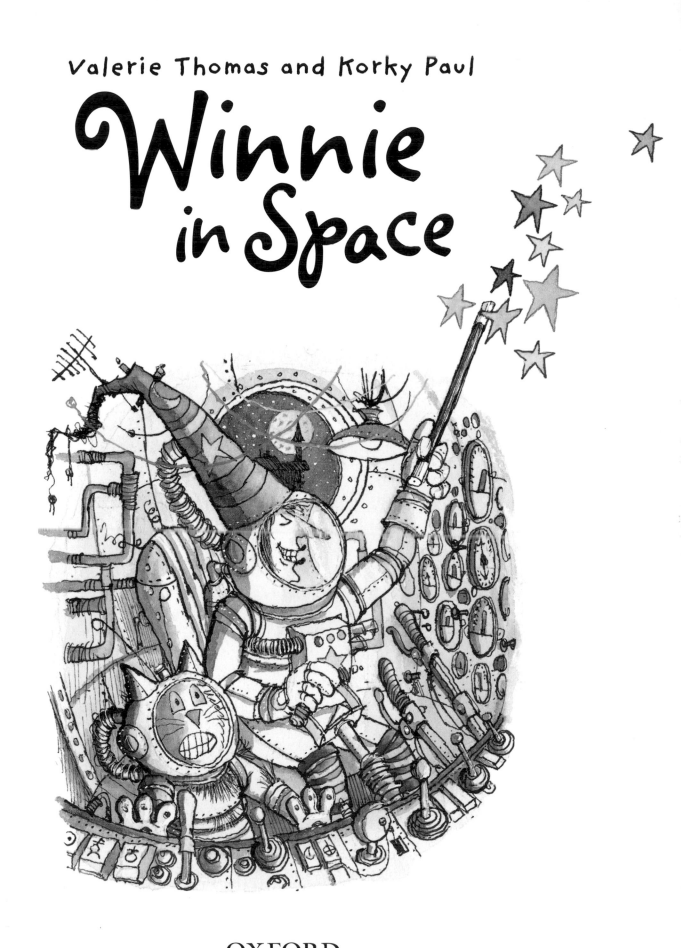

OXFORD

UNIVERSITY PRESS

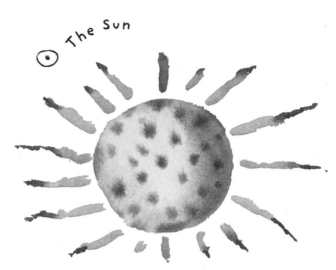

The Sun

Winnie the Witch loved to look through her telescope at the night sky.

It was huge and dark and mysterious. 'I'd love to go into space, Wilbur,' Winnie would say. 'It would be such a big adventure.'

Wilbur, Winnie's big black cat, loved to be outside at night too. He liked to chase moths and bats and shadows.

That was enough adventure for Wilbur.

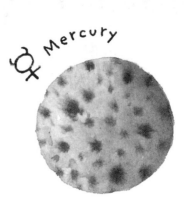

☿ Mercury

Then one night, when the Moon and stars were bright, Winnie suddenly said, 'Let's go into space right now, Wilbur!'

'**Meeow?**' said Wilbur.

'But how will we get there?' wondered Winnie. 'We need a rocket, and I don't have a rocket.' Then she looked up at the Moon, and she had a wonderful idea.

She waved her magic wand, shouted,

Abracadabra!

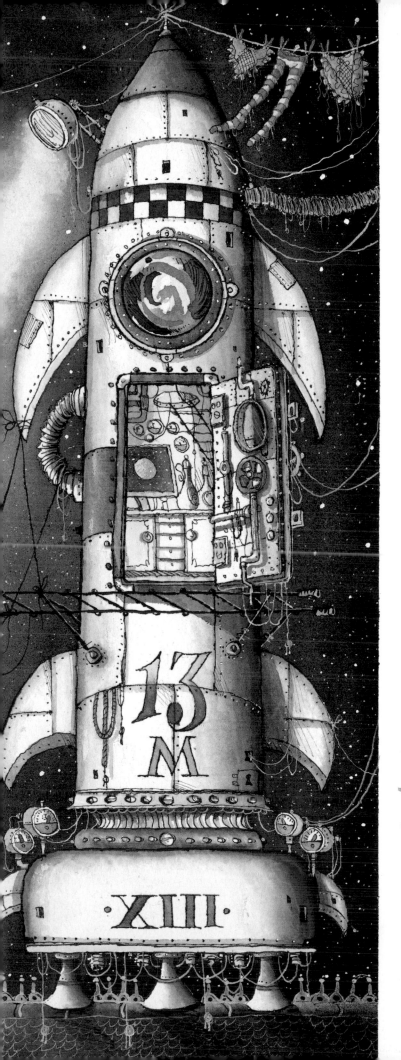

♀ Venus

... and there, on the roof, was a rocket. Winnie packed a picnic basket, got her Big Book of Spells, just in case, and ran up the stairs with Wilbur.

Winnie shut her eyes, waved her magic wand, and shouted,

Abracadabra!
10 9 8 7 6 5 4 ...

Earth

3 2 1 . . . .

The rocket shot off
the roof and into space.
It went very very fast.
And it was hard to steer.

'Oops!'
Winnie nearly flew
into a satellite.

'Oops!
That was a
falling star, Wilbur!'

'Oops!
Was that a
flying saucer?'

WHOOSH!

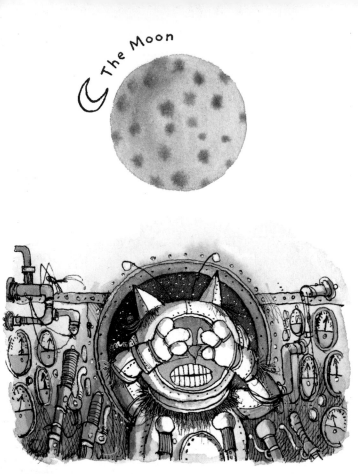

The Moon

'**Meeow!**' said Wilbur. He put his paws over his eyes.

'We'll find a lovely planet for our picnic, Wilbur,' Winnie said.

Wilbur peeped out from behind his paws. There were little planets everywhere.

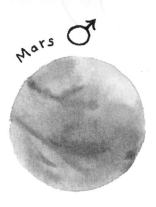

Mars ♂

'Here's a sweet little planet,' Winnie said. 'We'll have our picnic here.'

'**Purr!**' said Wilbur. He loved picnics.

PLOP! The rocket landed. All was quiet and peaceful. But there were funny little holes everywhere. Wilbur looked down the holes. They seemed to be empty . . .

Winnie unpacked the food. There were pumpkin scones, chocolate muffins, some cherries, and cream for Wilbur.

Yum!

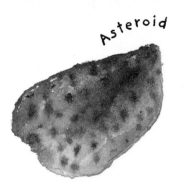

Asteroid

A little head popped out of a hole, and then there were heads everywhere.

'Rabbits!' said Winnie. 'Space rabbits are coming to our picnic!'

'Meeow!' said Wilbur.

A space rabbit hopped over to try some cream. Yuck!

Another space rabbit tried a pumpkin scone. Horrible.

Chocolate muffins? Disgusting. Cherries? Yuck!

Then some of the space rabbits
hopped over to the rocket.

They sniffed it . . .

♃ Jupiter

and took a bite. Then the rocket was covered in space rabbits.

'Oh no!' shouted Winnie. She waved her magic wand, shouted,

Abracadabra!

and carrots and lettuces rained down on the rabbits. But the space rabbits didn't like carrots or lettuces.

'Of course!' said Winnie. She waved her magic wand, shouted,

Abracadabra!

Saturn

. . . and there was a giant
pile of metal.

Saucepans,
wheelbarrows,
bicycles,
cars,
even a fire engine.

Yes! That was what
space rabbits liked.

Scrumptious!

But it was too late . . .

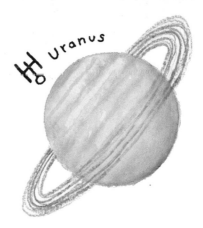

Uranus

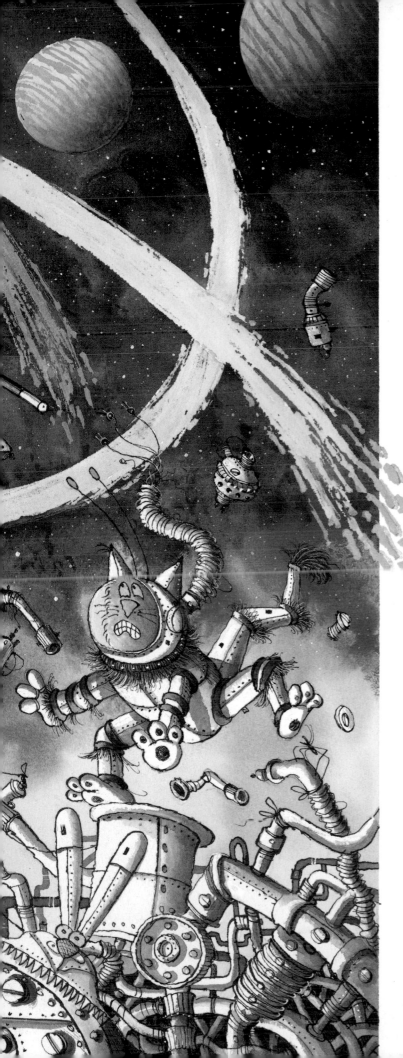

the space rabbits had eaten up all of Winnie's metal rocket.

'Blithering broomsticks!' shouted Winnie. 'Now how will we get home?'

'**Meeeow!**' said Wilbur.

Winnie looked at the giant pile of metal. 'Perhaps,' she said. 'Maybe. I wonder.'

She looked in her Big Book of Spells. 'Yes!' she said.

Then she picked up her magic wand, waved it five times, and shouted,

Abracadabra!

There was a flash of fire, a bang . . .

Neptune

and there, on top of the giant pile of metal, was a rattling, roaring scrap metal rocket.

Winnie and Wilbur climbed up to the rattling, roaring rocket and jumped in.

VROOM!
The rocket blasted away.
It rushed and roared
through space.

Pluto

WHUMP!

The rocket landed in Winnie's garden.

'That was an adventure, Wilbur,' Winnie said. 'But I'm glad we're home.'

'Purr, purr, purr,' said Wilbur.

He was very glad to be home.

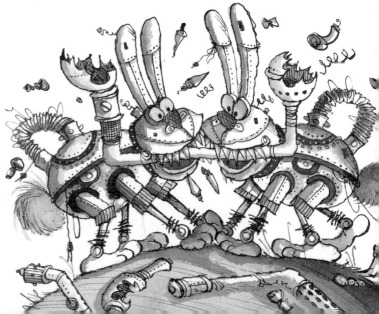

You probably know the names of
the nine planets in the solar system,
but can you remember the order
of the planets from the nearest to
the furthest from the Sun?

Winnie can help! Use her simple
mnemonic and you will never forget!

My	very	easy
☿	♀	⊕
Mercury	Venus	Earth

magic	just	simply
♂	♃	♄
Mars	Jupiter	Saturn

uses	nine	planets
♅	♆	♇
Uranus	Neptune	Pluto